Here I Am!

27.06.14

To our dear granddaughter Cleo

With best wishes

Gwilym Britt

To my lovely Grand Daughter
Cleo Vanessa
May you be as happy
caring for your child as I was for
your Mommy & siblings.

Love Nana Diane

LIBRARY AND ARCHIVES CANADA CATALOGUING IN PUBLICATION

Brott, Ardyth, 1951-
Here I Am! / written by Ardyth Brott ; illustrated by Dragana Miladinovic-Eic.

ISBN 978-0-88962-938-7

    1. Childbirth—Juvenile literature. 2. Newborn infants—Juvenile literature. 3. Newborn infants—Psychology-Juvenile literature. I. Miladinovic-Eic, Dragana, 1952- II. Title.

RJ251.B76 2011   j618.92'01   C2011-907077-4

Pubished by Mosaic Press, Oakville, Ontario, Canada, 2011. Distributed in Canada by Mosaic Press. Distributed in the United States by Midpoint Trade Books. Distributed in the U.K. by Gazelle Book Services.

MOSAIC PRESS, Publishers
Copyright © Ardyth Brot and Dragana Miladinovic-Eic, 2011
2nd printing, 2012
ISBN 978-0-88962-938-7
www.mosaic-press.com

WE ACKNOWLEDGE THE FINANCIAL SUPPORT OF THE GOVERNMENT OF CANADA THROUGH THE CANADA BOOK FUND (CBF) FOR THIS PROJECT.

NOUS RECONNAISSONS L'AIDE FINANCIÈRE DU GOUVERNEMENT DU CANADA PAR L'ENTREMISE DU FONDS DU LIVRE DU CANADA (FLC) POUR CE PROJET.

 Government of Canada   Gouvernement du Canada    Canada

Mosaic Press in Canada: 1252 Speers Road, Units 1 & 2
Oakville, Ontario L6L 5N9
Phone/Fax: 905-825-2130   info@mosaic-press.com

Mosaic Press in U.S.A.: c/o Livingston, 40 Sonwil Dr,
Cheektowaga, NY 14225
Phone/Fax: 905-825-2130   info@mosaic-press.com

Here I Am!

Written by Ardyth Brott

Illustrated Dragana Miladinovic-Eic

mosaic press

Soon I will be ready for the most important day of my life so far.

My birth!

I wonder how I know this?

I have been here for a long time.

I don't know how long it has been. Since forever, I think.

How long is forever?

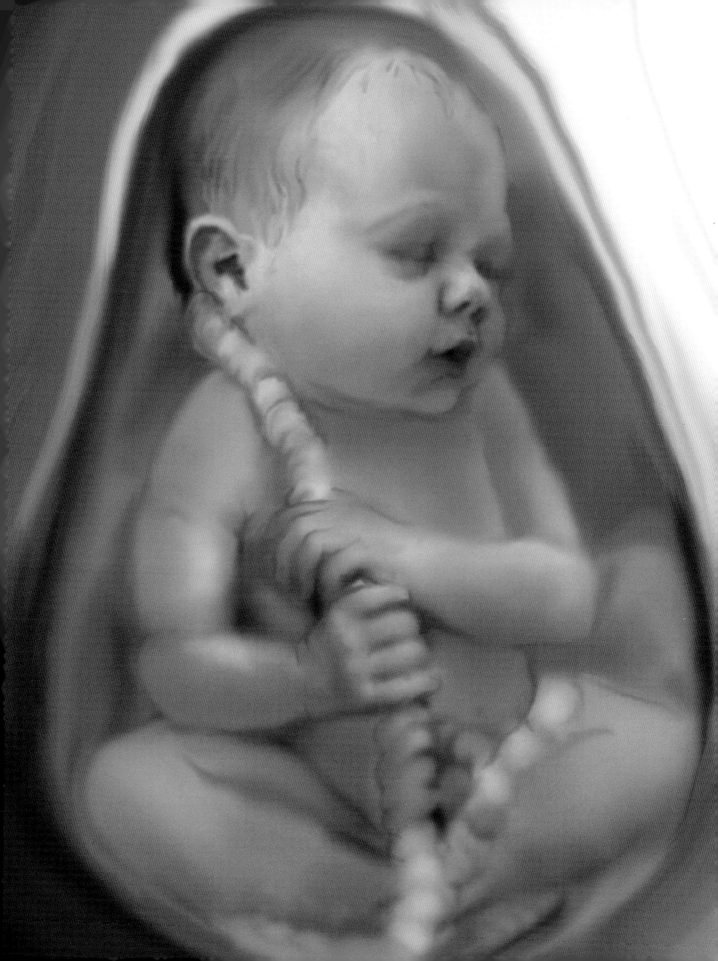

Sometimes I float around in Mommy's tummy.

Sometimes I bounce around as Mommy and Deep Voice go dancing.

Sometimes I sleep at the same time as Mommy sleeps.

Sometimes I do not sleep when Mommy sleeps.

Today, I made a very important discovery. I found my thumb.

I think I have two of them, and a whole bunch of fingers.

The fingers are different than my thumbs.

I can suck my thumb because it fits so perfectly into my mouth.

My mouth is another thing I found.
I can open it.

I don't know what good it is, other
than the thumb sucking part.

There is an *arf arf arf* sound. I wonder what that could be?

There is a *riinngg riinngg* sound. I wonder what that could be?

There is a *mmeeooww* sound. I wonder what that could be?

I also hear a *crunch crunch* sound and sometimes a *glug glug* sound.

Then all sorts of food and juice and water get washed down to the stomach.

I like that part. It is very exciting and very loud.

Sometimes I hear music and Mommy sings. I like that a lot. She has such a nice voice. She sings the same lullaby every day.

LaLa...Laaa. LaLa...Laaa. LaLa...La...La...lalala.

That song will be a part of me forever,
like my eyebrows or my toes or my thumbs.

The one sound I have heard since the beginning is Mommy's breathing.

I always hear the IN-OUT IN-OUT as the sound of air goes rushing past me.

Sometimes the Doctor listens to my heart beating. The Doctor even lets Mommy and Deep Voice listen. They get very excited. I don't know why they get so excited. I can hear Mommy's heartbeat all the time.

But here I am.

Waiting...

And waiting...

And waiting...

There is no room left. My Womb Room is too crowded. I wonder how that happened! I feel that everything is about to change. I think my big day, my Birth Day, will come soon.

I hope so. I have waited so long to see everybody.
I know so much about all of them and they know hardly anything about me.

I will be a surprise! A big surprise!

I am getting very tired.

I am going to have a long rest.

Mommy is tired too.

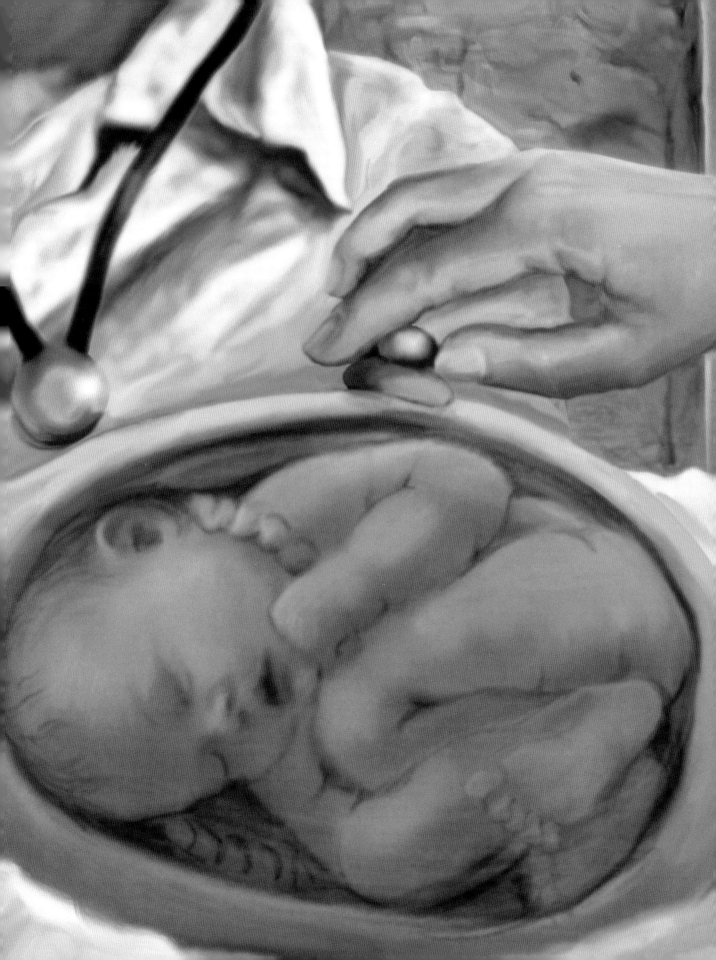

I will not kick her anymore.
Then something happens.
I am going down a long tunnel.

I am leaving my Womb Room.

Maybe this is my Birth Day.

Mommy's IN-OUT breathing
sounds different and she is
making the *Ooooo Ooooo*
sounds.

Then something at the top of my head feels different.

I am leaving my Womb Room.

I am born.

It is very exciting being born. I am carried through the tunnel.

It does not hurt, it just feels different. I feel the light against my eyes.

It is cold. I don't like cold. I was warm in my Womb Room.

Now I am not alone.
There are lots of voices.

People are saying to Mommy
and Deep Voice

"Congratulations. It's a girl/
boy."

I think that I should be
congratulated too. After all, I
had a very exciting journey.

I don't know what a girl/
boy is. I thought I was just a
person. I guess being a girl/
boy is OK.

My eyes are open now. I can see things that are dark and light.

The voices are louder. Much louder.

Now I am put on
Mommy's stomach.

I can still hear her breathing,
her heartbeat and the sound of
her voice.

Mommy and Deep voice are
counting my fingers and toes and
looking at every part of me.

They are smiling and crying and
laughing.

Now I am wrapped in a blanket.

Mommy is tired.

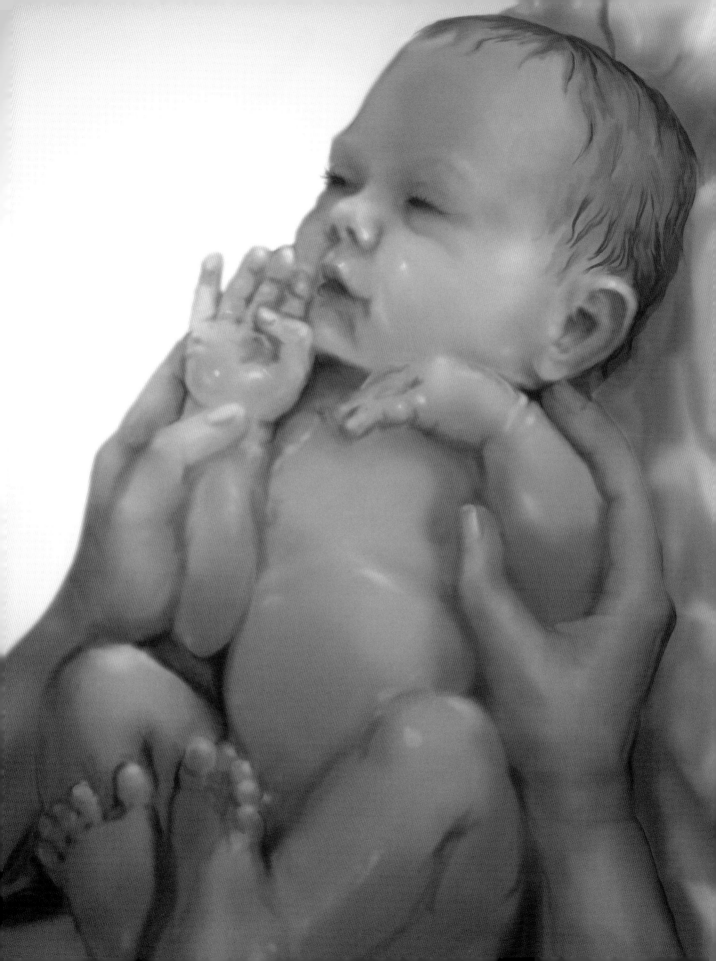

I am tired. I will go to sleep.

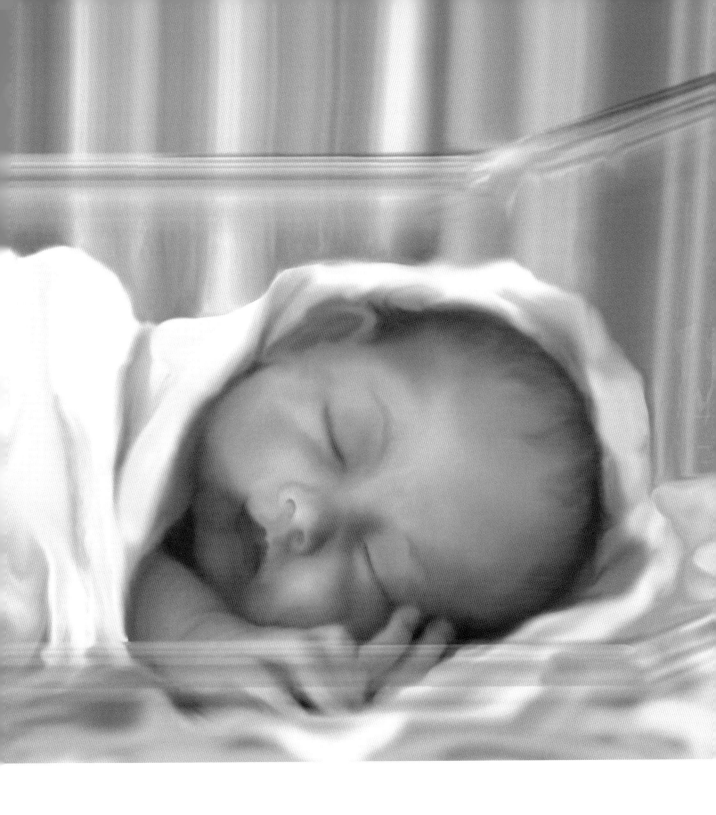

I have had a very big day.

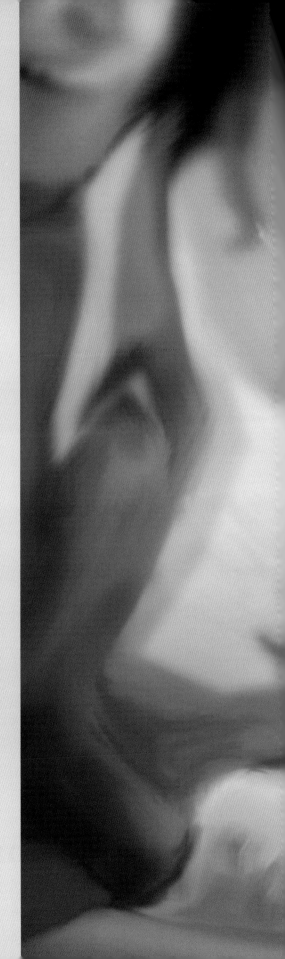

I am awake again. There are many faces looking at me. I can't see them very well. They are dark and light blobs. They are smiling and waving and saying:

I think s/he looks like

grandma/pa _____

Let's call her/him _____

I think s/he looks like

aunt/uncle _____

Let's call her/him _____

I think s/he looks like

cousin _____

Let's call her/him _____

Then Mommy and Deep Voice

Held me in their arms for a long time.

They looked and looked at me.

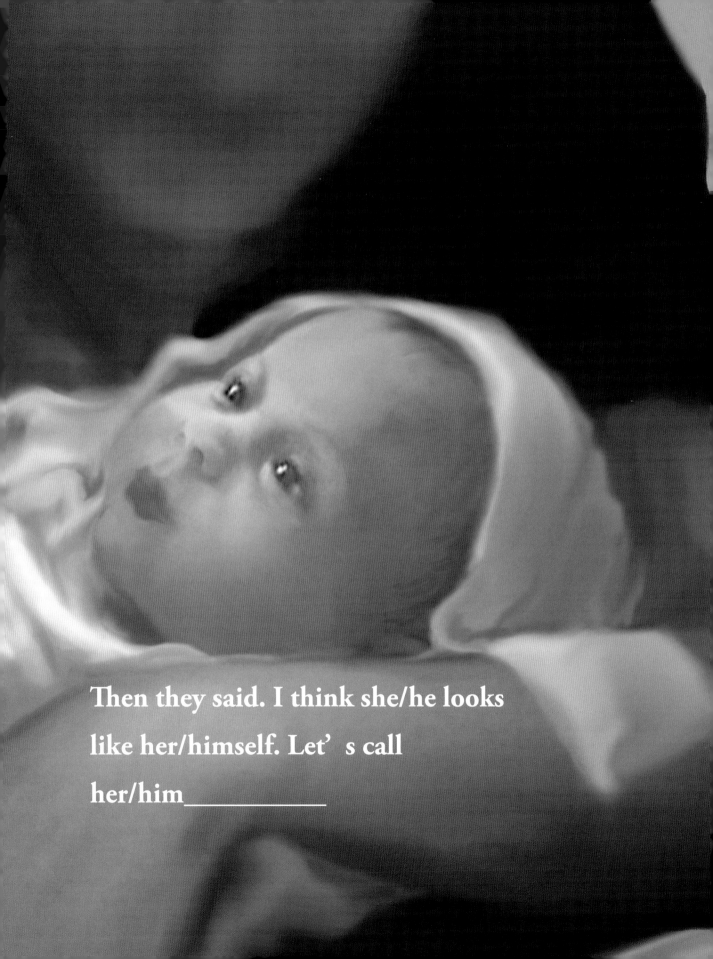

Then they said. I think she/he looks
like her/himself. Let's call
her/him_____

So, here I am, at last!

My name is _____

and I am a girl/boy.

Ardyth Brott is the author of the acclaimed children's book *Jeremy's Decision - Olivier Ne Sait Pas* and *The Loneliest Piano*. She is also a lawyer and an arts administrator. She makes her home in Hamilton and Montreal.

Dragana Miladinovic-Eic was born and raised in Kragujevac, Serbia, where she became fascinated with painting and sculpture during visits to her great aunt's art studio. She settled in Fredericton, NB in 1986 where she is an architect by profession, while pursuing her lifelong love of art. Her paintings are housed in private art collections in Canada, Europe and the United States.